With thanks to Erik

Library of Congress Control Number: 2008932788

ISBN: 978-0-8109-8926-9

Copyright © 2005 Uitgeverij Lannoo nv, Tielt

Original title: *Picknick met taart.* Translated from the Dutch language.

www.lannoo.com

English-language edition copyright © 2009 Harry N. Abrams, Inc.

Printed and bound in China

10 9 8 7 6 5 4 3 2 1

Abrams Books for Young Readers are available at special discounts when purchased in quantity
for premiums and promotions as well as fundraising or educational use. Special editions can also
be created to specification. For details, contact specialmarkets@hnabooks.com or the address below.

a subsidiary of La Martinière Groupe

115 West 18th Street

New York, NY 10011

www.hnabooks.com

Where Is the Cake Now?

T. T. Khing

Abrams Books for Young Readers
New York